To Abel -
No matter what feelings change,
my love for you is infinite

Merry Christmas 2019   ♡ Auntie Emily

Maybe

A Little Zen for Little Ones™

By

Sanjay Nambiar

Maybe

Published by Umiya Publishing.
www.umiyapublishing.com

For the book series: www.alittlezen.com.

Edited by Priya Nambiar.
Illustrated by 3-Keys Graphics and Printing.

First edition | 10 9 8 7 6 5 4 3 2 1
ISBN 978-0-9838243-0-5
Library of Congress Control Number 2011938095

Printed in China.

This book will receive loving kindness from

ADEL

A gentle, kind girl
lived with her family

in a friendly neighborhood and loving home.

One day, her bicycle disappeared.

Her friends said,
"That's terrible luck! You had such a nice bike.
What a bummer!"

The thoughtful girl
took a moment,
and then responded,

"Maybe."

The girl was getting too big for her old bicycle anyway. So, her parents bought her a new one.

It was a beautiful shade of blue
and looked like a treasure on wheels.

"What an awesome bike,"
exclaimed her friends.
"You are so lucky!"

"Maybe,"
said the wise girl.

A week later, the girl was riding her bicycle and hit a bump in the road.

She fell hard to the ground and hurt her arm.

There were scratches and bruises,
and even a little blood.

As she rested in bed to heal the injuries,
her friends visited her.
They said, "Oh, those bruises look awful.
That's really bad luck you had with that new bike!"

She just smiled and replied,
"Maybe."

The next day, the kids in the neighborhood went to school as usual.

The girl, however, stayed home.

She read books all day.

Her mother made her favorite meal,
vegetable lasagna.

The neighborhood kids visited her after school and learned about her special day.
They said, "Wow, you got to skip school and had so much fun at home! You're so lucky!"

The girl looked at her friends and smiled gently.
"Maybe," she said.

The girl's arm was not yet healed, and she stayed at home for another day.

This time, one of the kids at school celebrated his birthday.

Everyone enjoyed cake and hot chocolate.

When the kids in the neighborhood visited the kind girl after school, they said, "You totally missed out today! We had the most delicious cake and the birthday party was fantastic. You had some bad luck."

The wise girl did not feel bad about missing the party.
She just gave her usual reply,

"Maybe."

That night, the kids in the neighborhood
had a restless sleep – the cake had a lot of sugar
and gave all the kids a tummy ache.

The following morning, the kind girl felt better and went to school. All her friends were tired and miserable; they had spent the whole night feeling sick to their stomachs. They looked at the girl and said, "You're so lucky you didn't have that cake. That was the worst tummy ache ever!"

The girl chuckled and
said with a big smile,

"Maybe."

A Brief Explanation

Hi Kids! Did you know this story is based on an ancient Zen fable? In the fable, a farmer experiences a bunch of events that at first seem lucky (or unlucky) but then turn out to be quite the opposite. It's a very old and beautiful story, but the ideas and lessons are just as important in today's world.

So, why do you think the girl in our book keeps saying, "Maybe?" Here are some of our ideas . . .

We often think about things that happen to us as "lucky" or "unlucky." We can get caught up in the emotion of the moment and rush to feel sad or happy. But, soon enough, what we thought was great (or bad) leads to something else that we couldn't even imagine at first.

This story shows how we can greatly benefit by not focusing on the emotion of any single event. If something bad (or good) happens, we never know what will happen next. What we thought was horribly "unlucky" could turn out to be a wonderful blessing.

When something happens, the wise girl in this story doesn't get carried away in the drama of the moment. She stays calm and peaceful. Was what happened good luck? Maybe. Was it bad luck? Maybe. Really, it was just a single event, and she doesn't place any judgment around it. Because we never know what that event might lead to, "good" or "bad" . . .

These are just a few ways to interpret the story. What are your ideas?

Color me!